How To Nab
A Rabbit

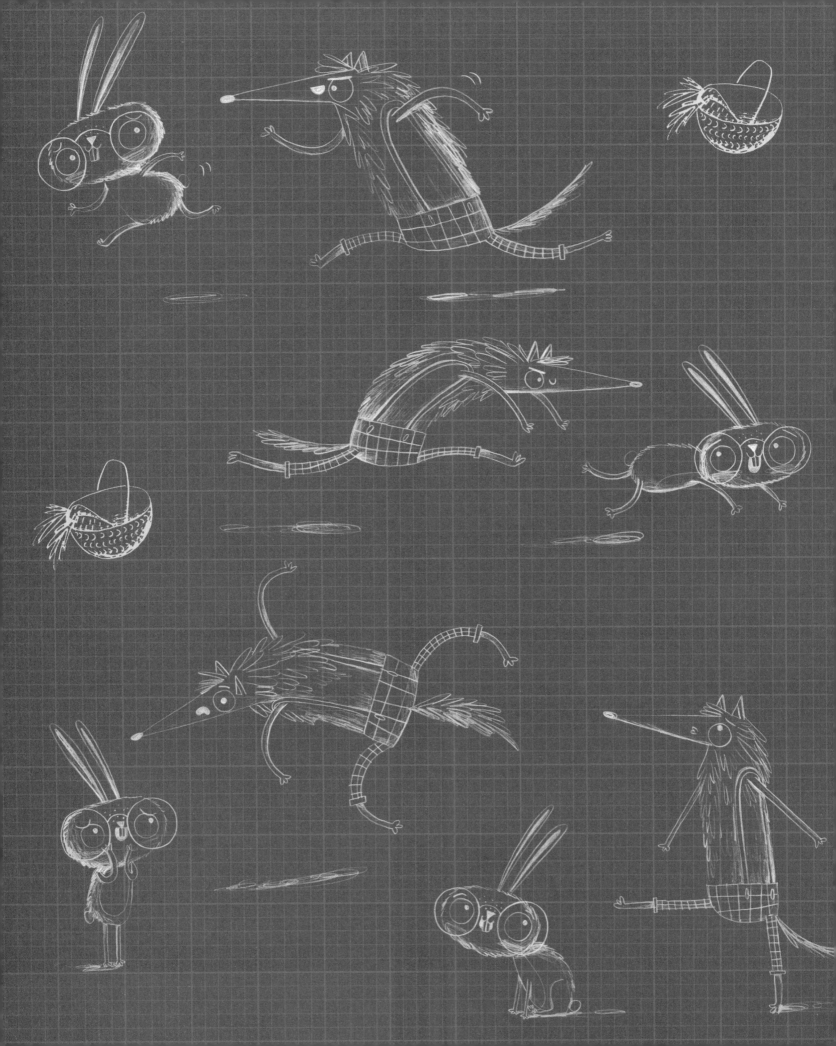

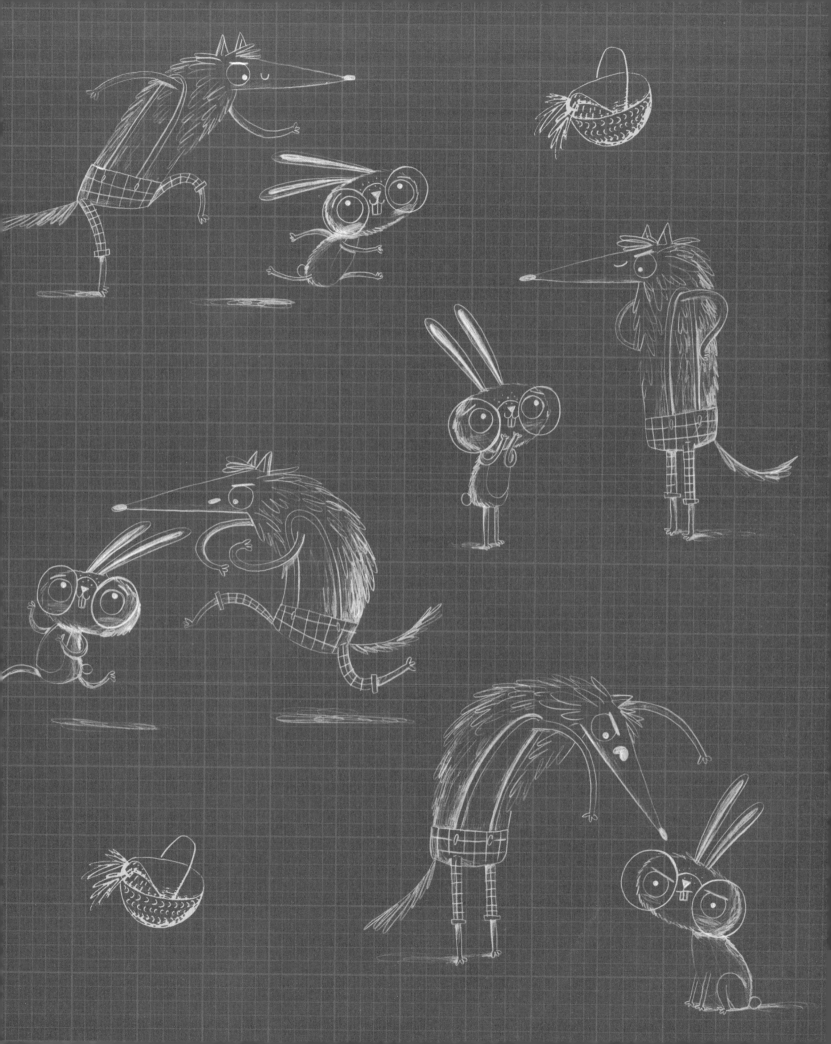

For Michael with love – CF

For Stasiu – MF

SIMON & SCHUSTER
First published in Great Britain in 2018 by Simon & Schuster UK Ltd
1st Floor, 222 Gray's Inn Road, London, WC1X 8HB • A CBS Company
Text copyright © 2018 Claire Freedman • Illustrations copyright © 2018 Monika Filipina
The right of Claire Freedman and Monika Filipina to be identified as the author and
illustrator of this work has been asserted by them in accordance with the Copyright,
Designs and Patents Act, 1988 • All rights reserved, including the right of reproduction in
whole or in part in any form • A CIP catalogue record for this book is available from the
British Library upon request.
978-1-4711-4450-9 (HB) • 978-1-4711-4451-6 (PB) • 978-1-4711-4452-3 (eBook)
Printed in China • 10 9 8 7 6 5 4 3 2 1

How To Nab A Rabbit

by the Big Bad Wolf

(Absolutely foolproof) hardy

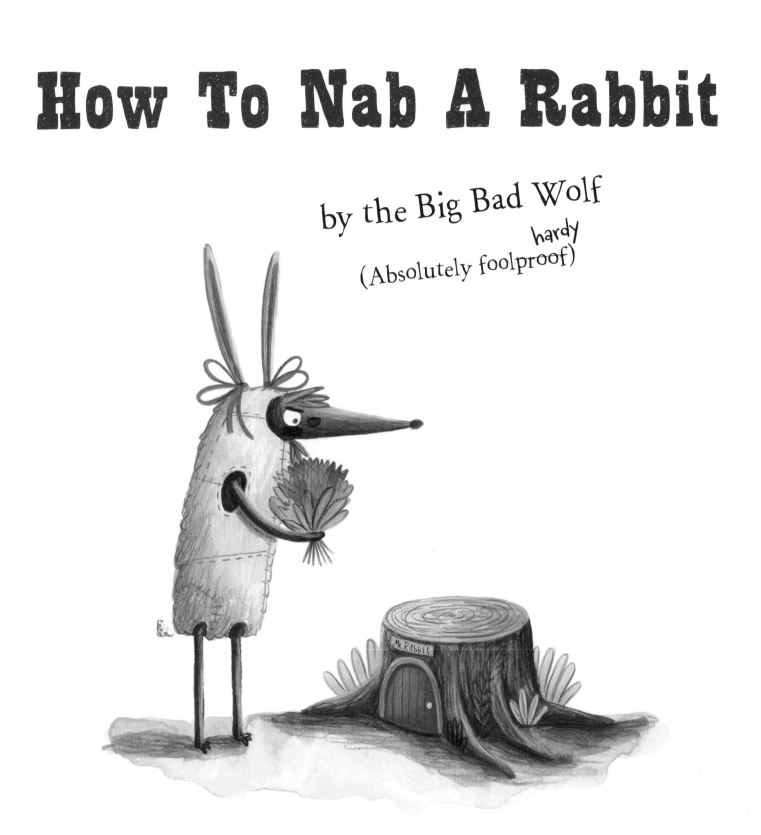

Claire Freedman and Monika Filipina

SIMON & SCHUSTER

London   New York   Sydney   Toronto   New Delhi

Hello, wolf friends!
It's ME – the famous Big Bad Wolf.
Having problems catching pesky rabbits?

Well, no longer! I proudly
present my brilliant book.

How to
nab
a rAbbit
BiG BAD
Wolf

It's life-changing!

How To Nab a Rabbit

For hungry wolves, this book is a winner,
It shows you how to catch your dinner.
Love bunny pie and rabbit stew?
They'll soon become your dream come true.

These easy tips are all foolproof,
Revealed by me – the Big Bad Wolf!

By the way, wolf friends,
To illustrate my rabbit hunts,
I'll demonstrate some daring stunts!
Let me show you . . .

THE STALKING STRATEGY

First things first, you locate their lair,
Those rabbits can lurk everywhere!
Most love to hide, so you must think smart,
Deep down in the woods is the place to start.

To catch your lunch you must be sly,

So just pretend you're passing by . . .

DRAT!

Pesky rabbits are smarter than they look!

VERY IMPORTANT FACT:

Bears ALSO hang out in the woods,
And think that wolves make tasty puds.

Let's move on . . .

THE HOLE-IN-THE-GROUND HOAX

Dig a deep hole so your supper falls in,
Cover with twigs and it won't see a THING!

IMPORTANT HINT:

When you've dug your pit,
Be sure that YOU don't land in it!

Can't anybody hear me shout?
Help! I'm stuck!
Please get me out!

YIKES!

Mr Bear! Oh, trust my luck!
I think I'd rather stay here, stuck!

This next idea will DEFINITELY work!
No danger! What could possibly go wrong?

THE LOVE LURE

FoR RomAnTics

1. Sew a bunny-suit

2. Add a ribbon or two

3. Fool a bunny to fall in love with you!

Just play along and he'll never tell.

(Beware! This tip might work TOO well!)

BLEARGH!

I hope my friends can't see
A bunny rabbit kissing me!

Oh no!
Not him . . . !

Please tell me I won't get kissed by a BEAR?
I'm not a bunny! I'm not a bunny! I'm not a bunny!

Right, wolf friends, it's true we've had a few hiccups so far,
but my next idea is totally idiot-proof!

THE POSTMAN PLOY

Mr. Rabbit
12 THE BuRRoWs
MeAdoWLahE

If you are small and light to lift,
Post yourself as his birthday gift,

Surprise your bunny when the postman knocks,
But don't get stuck in the letterbox!

What do you mean 'the WRONG address'?
Oh yikes, I'm in an awful mess!

IMPORTANT:
Do not accidentally post yourself
to that horrible Bear's house.

YEE-OUCH!

This next one MUST succeed. My reputation depends on it!

SPRING INTO ACTION

Pesky rabbits can hop SO fast,
Before you've caught them,
They've bounced right past,
So find a nice big metal spring,
Attach – to give you 'go fast' zing!

Oh no . . .

P.S. If you've tried these steps with no success,
And sadly made a total mess,

There's one last thing I suggest you do –
Go home and cook some vegetable stew!

YUM! Surprisingly tasty, wolf friends!

In fact, that's given me an idea for a fantastic NEW book!

How to be a Vegetarian

For hungry wolves, this book is a winner,
It shows you how to COOK your dinner.
Spuds, carrots, leeks, big turnips too,
Will soon become your dream come true.

These recipes are all foolproof,
Prepared by me – the Big Bad Wolf!

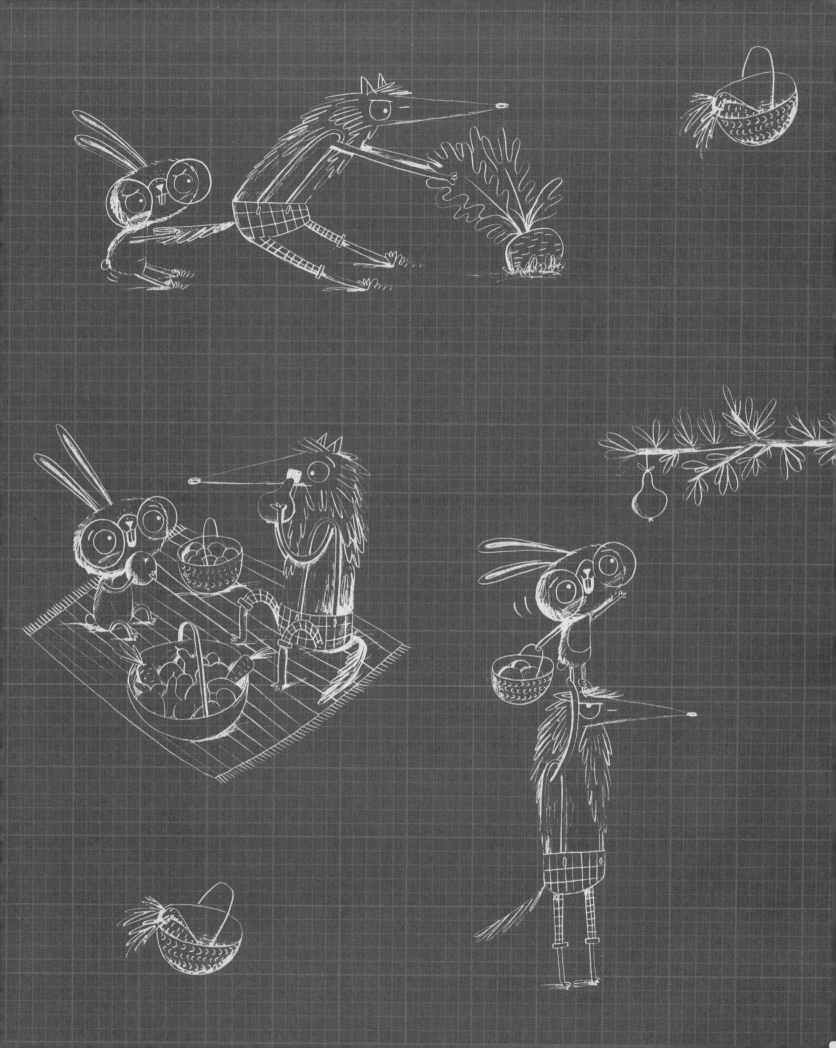